A catalogue record for this book is available from the British Library

Published by Ladybird Books Ltd  Loughborough  Leicestershire  UK
Ladybird Books Ltd is a subsidiary of the Penguin Group of companies
Text © Tony Bradman MCMXCVI  Illustrations © Adrienne Geoghegan MCMXCVI
The author/artist have asserted their moral rights
LADYBIRD and the device of a Ladybird are trademarks of Ladybird Books Ltd

# Pushchair Polly

by Tony Bradman
*illustrated by* Adrienne Geoghegan

Polly loved her pushchair.

She loved its handles and its comfy seat…

its buckle-up belt and the bar where
she put her feet.

Polly loved every squeak of its fat
little wheels.

Polly sat in it for most of her meals...
for breakfast, for lunch, for dinner.

She rode in it...

played in it...

sang in it.

She spent most of every day in it.

Polly sat in her pushchair for watching
TV, and brushing her teeth, and having
stories. If she could, Polly would have
made it her bed.

"We'll have to call you...
*Pushchair Polly!*" Mum and Dad said.

Polly didn't mind that. In fact, she rather liked the name. And everything would have been fine and dandy but… things never stay the same.

For – without her knowing – Polly was
**grow*ing*** and growing...

One day she looked down and saw that her feet didn't fit on the bar any more.

Her buckle-up belt felt tight, too. And she was still **growing**...

She noticed her bottom wasn't comfy in the seat any more. The fat little wheels didn't squeak – they groaned. And she was still **growing**...

Polly had to fold herself in but, once
she had, it was very hard to get out!
Polly wanted to scream and shout.
And she was *still* grow**ing**...

Soon Polly's knees were up near her ears. All Polly could do now was burst into tears! She wouldn't be Pushchair Polly any more.

Polly felt sad. So Mum and Dad took her out for a treat. On the way back they went past a shop, where Polly stopped and stared.

She'd seen something she liked –
a magnificent bike!

And that's what she got for her birthday!
Polly loved the spin of its silvery wheels.

She loved its handles and its comfy seat…

its ring-a-ding bell and the pedals where she put her feet.

Polly sat on it for most of
her meals... for breakfast...

for lunch...

for dinner.

She rode on it, sang on it, played on it.
She spent most of every day on it.

Polly sat on her bike for watching TV, and brushing her teeth, and having stories. If she could, Polly would have kept it by her bed.

"We'll have to call you…
*Pushbike Polly!*" Mum and Dad said.

Polly didn't mind that. In fact, she liked the name, and now she was as happy as could be. So off she flew with a…

"*Wheeeeee…*"

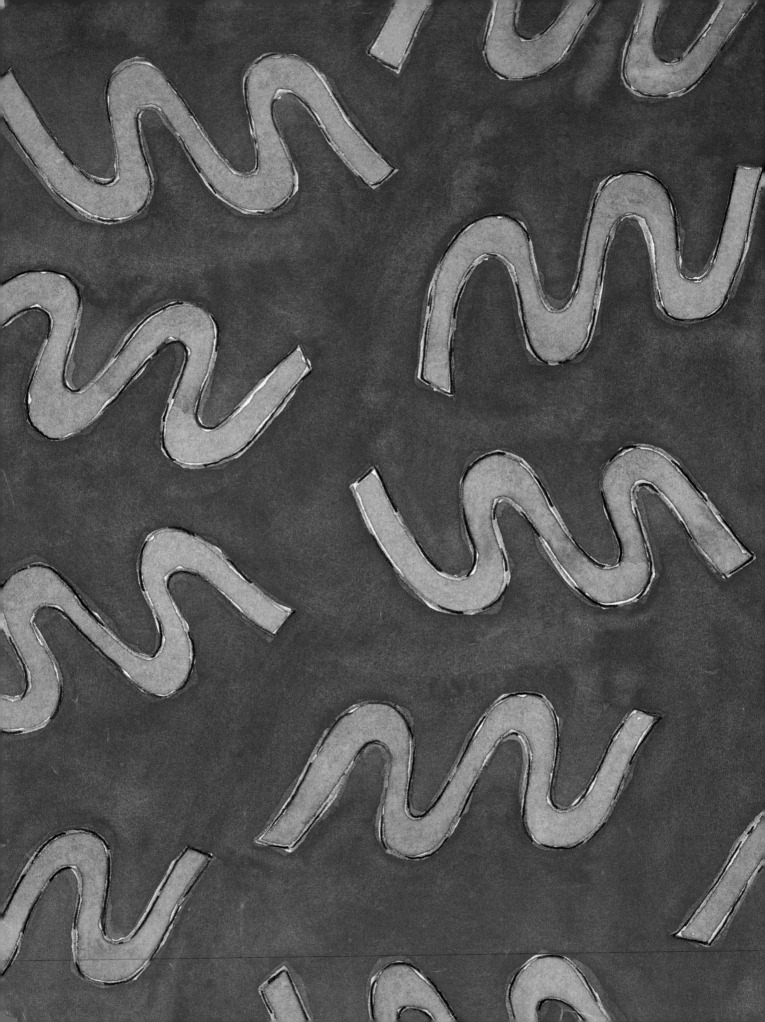

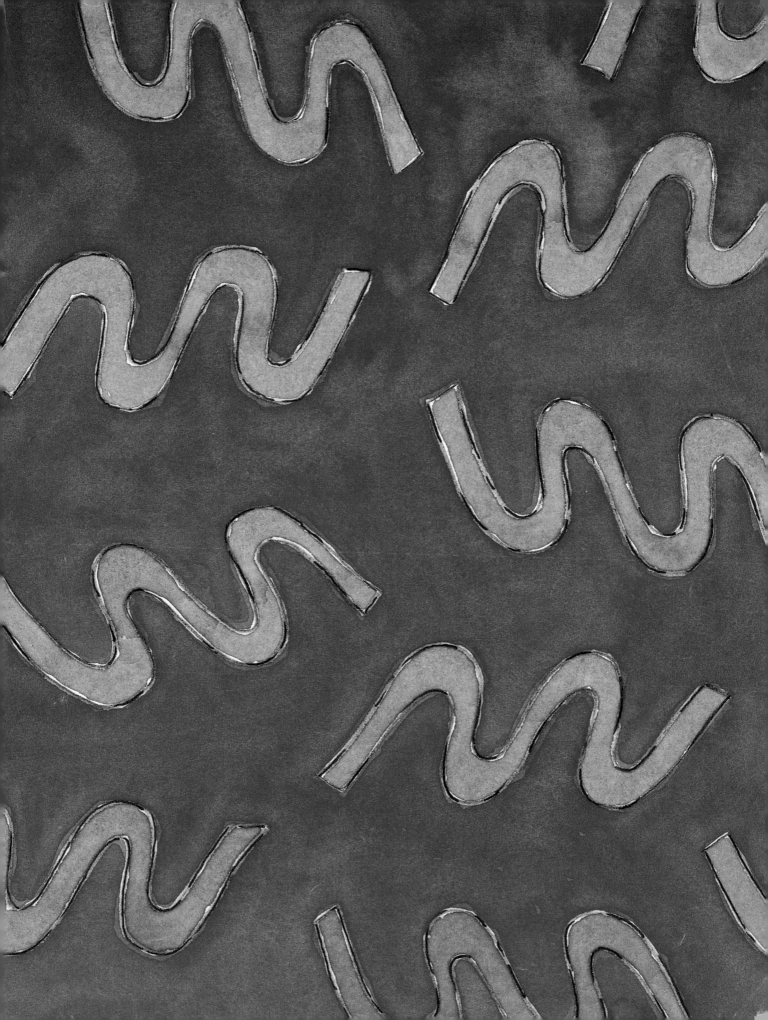

# Picture Ladybird

### Books for reading aloud with 2 – 6 year olds

The exciting *Picture Ladybird* series includes a wide range
of animal stories, funny rhymes, and real life adventures that are
perfect to read aloud and share at storytime or bedtime.

## A whole library of beautiful books for you to collect

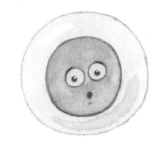

### RHYMING STORIES

Easy to follow and great for joining in!

*Jasper's Jungle Journey*, Val Biro
*Shoo Fly, Shoo!* Brian Moses
*Ten Tall Giraffes*, Brian Moses
*In Comes the Tide*, Valerie King
*Toot! Learns to Fly*,
Geraldine Taylor & Jill Harker
*Who Am I?* Judith Nicholls
*Fly Eagle, Fly!* Jan Pollard

### IMAGINATIVE TALES

Mysterious and magical, or just a little shivery

*The Star that Fell*, Karen Hayles
*Wishing Moon*, Lesley Harker
*Don't Worry William*, Christine Morton
*This Way Little Badger*, Phil McMylor
*The Giant Walks*, Judith Nicholls
*Kelly and the Mermaid*, Karen King

### FUNNY STORIES

Make storytime good fun!

*Benedict Goes to the Beach*, Chris Demarest
*Bella and Gertie*, Geraldine Taylor
*Edward Goes Exploring*, David Pace
*Telephone Ted*, Joan Stimson
*Top Shelf Ted*, Joan Stimson
*Helpful Henry*, Shen Roddie
*What's Wrong with Bertie?* Tony Bradman
*Bears Can't Fly*, Val Biro
*Finnigan's Flap*, Joan Stimson

### REAL LIFE ADVENTURE

Situations to explore and discover

*Joe and the Farm Goose*,
Geraldine Taylor & Jill Harker
*Going to Playgroup*,
Geraldine Taylor & Jill Harker
*The Great Rabbit Race*, Geraldine Taylor
*Pushchair Polly*, Tony Bradman

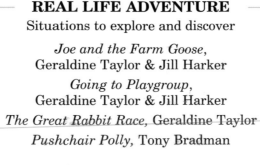